My
Dancing

For Oscar Branson
K.W.

For Lynne
A.J.

First published 1993
by Walker Books Ltd
87 Vauxhall Walk
London SE11 5HJ

This edition published 2010

10 9 8 7 6 5 4 3 2 1

Text © 1993 Karen Wallace
Illustrations © 1993 Anita Jeram

The moral rights of the author
and illustrator have been asserted

This book has been typeset in
Bembo Educational

Printed in China

British Library Cataloguing in Publication Data:
a catalogue record for this book is available from
the British Library

ISBN 978-1-4063-1862-3

www.walker.co.uk

My Hen Is Dancing

Karen Wallace

illustrated by

Anita Jeram

WALKER BOOKS
AND SUBSIDIARIES
LONDON · BOSTON · SYDNEY · AUCKLAND

My hen is dancing
in the farmyard.

She takes two
steps forward

and one
step back.

She bends her
neck and
pecks and
scratches.

Her beak snaps
shut. She's found
a worm.

My hen is rolling in her dustbath.

She likes the ground when it's gritty
and dry.

She cleans her feathers with her
beak and scratches her ears with
her toenails.

She stretches her wings and
sleeps in the sun.

My hen never struggles if you hold her.

Her feathers
are long and
smooth on
her wings.

Underneath she's soft like
a feather duster.
Her bones feel hard like
thin sticks inside her.

My hen lives in a
henhouse with five
other hens.

There's fresh straw on the floor

and a row of nestboxes along the back wall.

A cockerel lives there too. He has
shiny tail feathers and a red coxcomb
like a crown.

If my hen wanders, he brings her home.

My hen lays big brown eggs. When there are chicks growing inside them, she sits in her nestbox and puffs up her feathers.

18

She pecks you if you try to
touch them.

 Her  chicks are wet an wet an

They creep underneath her

sticky when they hatch.

where she's fluffy and warm.

My hen leads her chicks around
the farmyard.

They learn to scratch

and peck   and pull worms

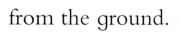

from the ground.

My hen knows when it's time to go to sleep. As soon as it gets dark, she hops into the henhouse.

She sleeps standing up. Her long toes grip the perch so she doesn't fall.

We close the henhouse door at night
to keep her safe from hungry foxes.

In the morning I open the door.
The cockerel jumps out with my
hen close behind him.

The cockerel
crows and she
steps up beside
him.

My hen is dancing in the farmyard.

More about hens

Hens eat all kinds of things, including corn, crumbs, worms, insects, grass and vegetable scraps.

A hen doesn't have teeth. Food goes down into a pouch in her body to be softened, then into her gizzard, where it's ground up by the bits of grit she swallows.

A hen can't fly far because her wings aren't strong, but she can flutter up and down from a perch.

Dustbaths are good for cleaning feathers and controlling fleas.

A hen also preens herself every day with oil. It comes from where her tail feathers grow, and she picks it up and spreads it with her beak.

Sleeping like this is called "roosting".

Some kinds of hen lay brown eggs. Some kinds of hen lay white eggs. No kind of hen lays both.

A hen's chicks take three weeks to hatch. She sits on the eggs, turning them every day so that they stay warm all over.

While she is sitting on her eggs, she is called a "broody" hen.

A newborn chick needs the warmth of its mother to survive.

It takes about six months for a chick to grow into a hen or a cockerel.

Different kinds of hens

Black Leghorn

White Frizzle

Welsummer

Warren Hybrid (my hen)

Silver-spangled Hamburg

White Transylvanian Naked-ne

Buff-laced Wyandotte

White-crested Black Poland

Light Sussex

Maran

White Plymouth Rock

Silver Duckwing Old English Game

Index

About the Author

Karen Wallace was raised in a log
cabin in the woods of Quebec, but
now lives in Herefordshire. She has
won awards on both sides of the
Atlantic and writes television scripts
in addition to children's books.

About the Illustrator

Anita Jeram studied art in
Manchester, and now lives in
Northern Ireland with her husband,
who studies animal and plant fossils,
and their three children.

There are 10 titles in the
READ AND DISCOVER series.
Which ones have you read?

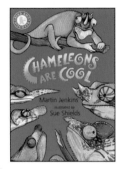
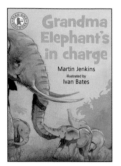
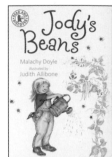

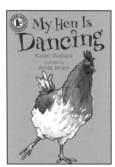

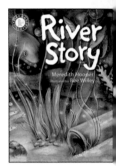

Available from all good booksellers

www.walker.co.uk

FOR THE BEST CHILDREN'S BOOKS, LOOK FOR THE BEAR.